Arranged for all portable keyboards *by Kenneth Baker.*

THE COMPLETE KEYBOARD PLAYER
EASY LISTENING

GW00417551

Wise Publications
London/New York/Sydney

Exclusive Distributors:
Music Sales Limited
8/9 Frith Street, London W1V 5TZ, England.
Music Sales Pty Limited
120 Rothschild Avenue, Rosebery, NSW 2018, Australia.

This book © Copyright 1991 by Wise Publications
Order No.AM84765
UK ISBN 0.7119.2648.4

Designed by Pearce Marchbank Studio
Arranged by Kenneth Baker
Compiled by Peter Evans
Music processed by Bill Pitt Musical Services

Photographs courtesy of:
London Features International

Music Sales' complete catalogue lists thousands of
titles and is free from your local music shop,
or direct from Music Sales Limited.
Please send a cheque or postal order for £1.50 for postage to
Music Sales Limited, Newmarket Road, Bury St. Edmunds, Suffolk IP33 3YB.

Printed in the United Kingdom by
J.B. Offset Printers (Marks Tey) Limited, Marks Tey, Essex.

I'LL KNOW

Words and Music by Frank Loesser

Suggested registration: clarinet
Rhythm: bossa nova
Tempo: medium (♩ = 92)

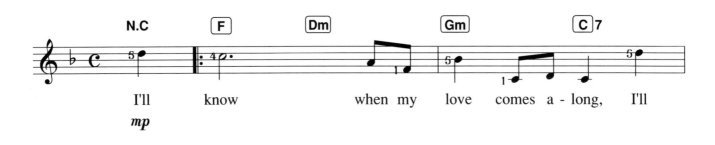

I'll know when my love comes a-long, I'll
mp

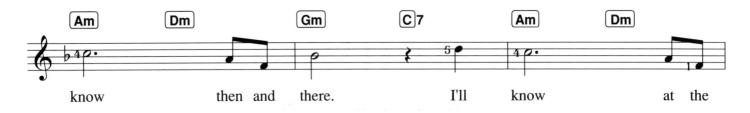

know then and there. I'll know at the

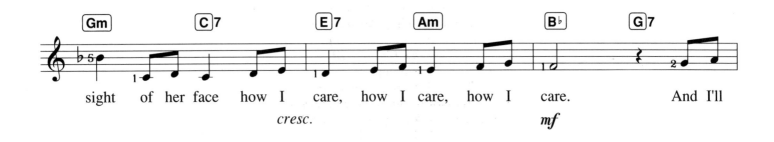

sight of her face how I care, how I care, how I care. And I'll
cresc. *mf*

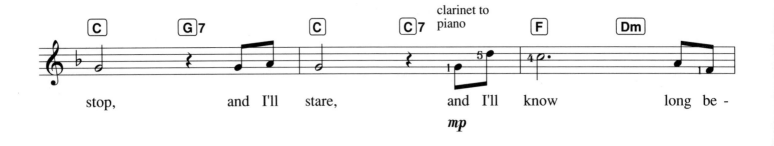

clarinet to piano
stop, and I'll stare, and I'll know long be-
mp

fore we can speak, I'll know in my heart, I'll

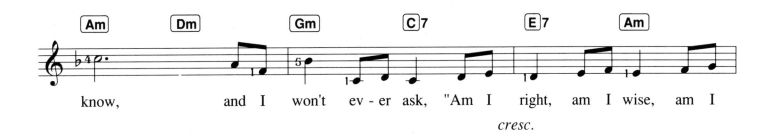

know,   and I   won't   ev - er   ask, "Am I   right,   am I   wise,   am I

cresc.

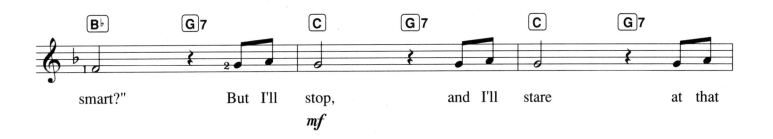

smart?"   But I'll   stop,   and I'll   stare   at that

mf

Piano to clarinet

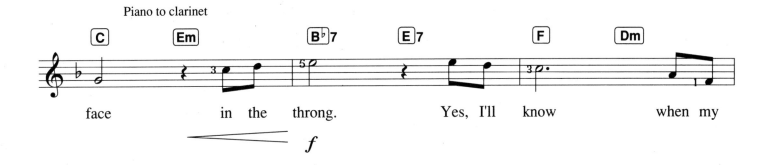

face   in the   throng.   Yes, I'll   know   when my

f

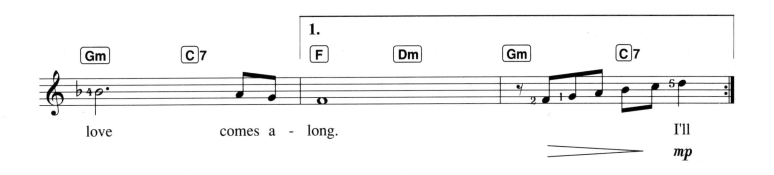

love   comes a - long.   I'll

mp

long.   stop rhythm

PORTRAIT OF MY LOVE

Words by David West
Music by Cyril Ornadel

Suggested registration: oboe
Rhythm: bossa nova
Tempo: medium (♩ = 100)

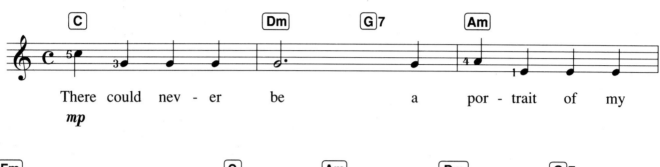

There could nev-er be a por-trait of my
mp

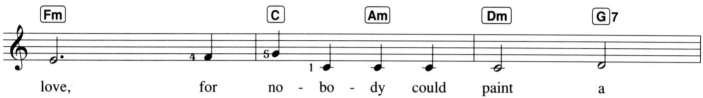

love, for no-bo-dy could paint a

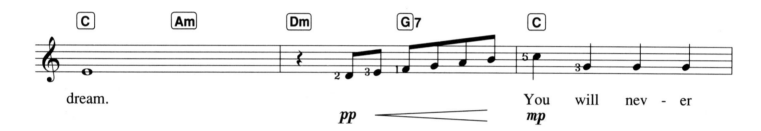

dream. You will nev-er
pp *mp*

see a por-trait of my love, for

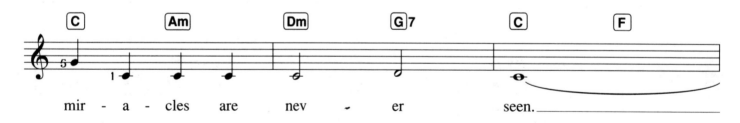

mir-a-cles are nev-er seen.____

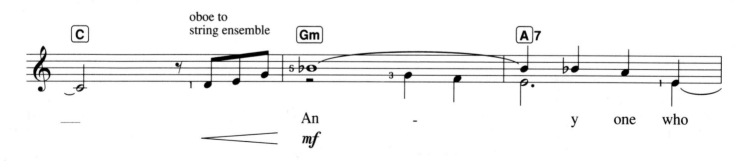

oboe to
string ensemble

An - y one who
mf

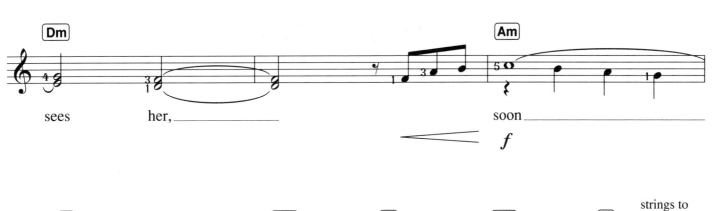

sees   her,_____   soon_____

f

___ for - gets   the   Mo - na   Li - sa.

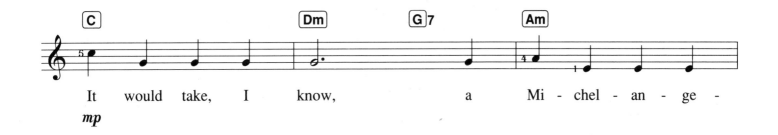

It   would   take,   I   know,   a   Mi - chel - an - ge -

mp

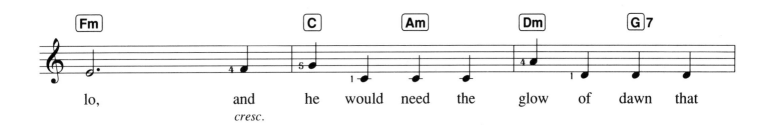

lo,   and   he   would   need   the   glow   of   dawn   that

cresc.

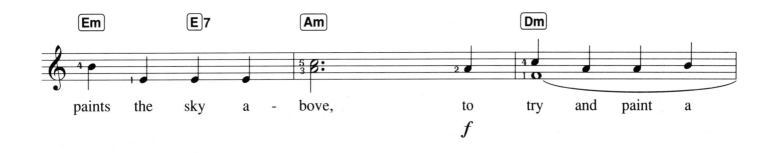

paints   the   sky   a - bove,   to   try   and   paint   a

f

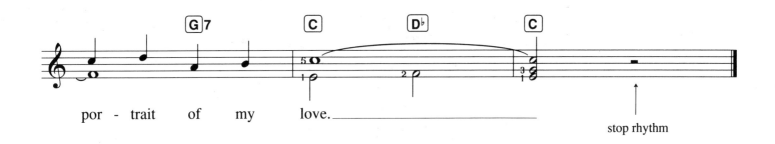

por - trait   of   my   love._____

stop rhythm

WITHOUT YOU

Words & Music by Peter Ham & Tom Evans

Suggested registration: vibes
Rhythm: rock
Tempo: slow (♩ = 76)

No, I can't for-get this ev-'ning, or your face as you were leav-ing, but I

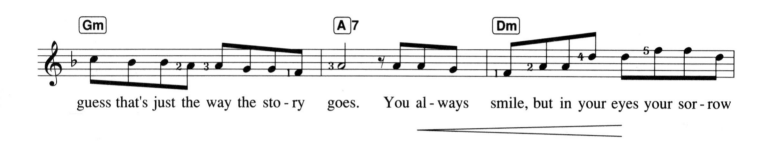

guess that's just the way the sto-ry goes. You al-ways smile, but in your eyes your sor-row

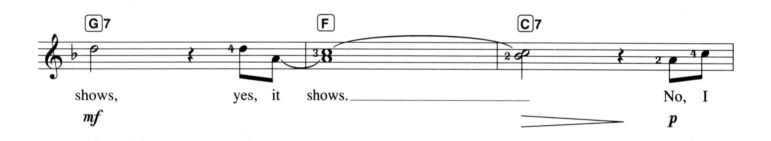

shows, yes, it shows._____ No, I

can't for-get to-mor-row when I think of all my sor-row, and I had you there, but then I let you

go.   And now it's on - ly fair that I should let you know   what you should

mf

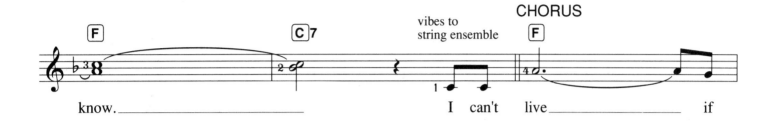

vibes to
string ensemble

CHORUS

know._____   I can't live_____ if

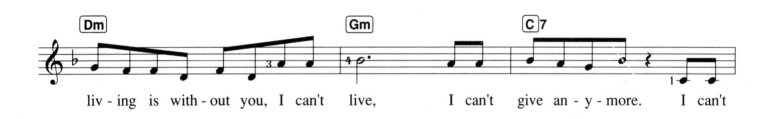

liv - ing is with - out you, I can't live,   I can't give an - y - more.   I can't

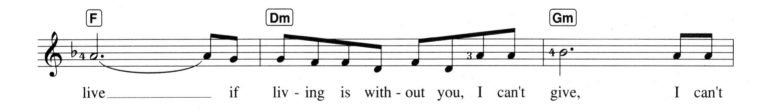

live_____   if liv - ing is with - out you, I can't give,   I can't

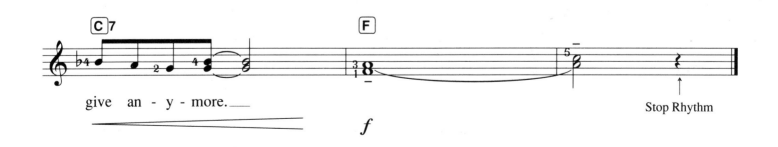

give an - y - more.____   Stop Rhythm

f

WONDERFUL TONIGHT

Words& Music by Eric Clapton

Suggested registration: guitar
Rhythm: rock
Tempo: medium (♩ = 108)

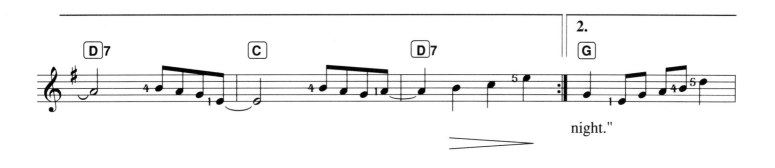

2.

night."

INTERLUDE

I feel won - der - ful___ be - cause I see___ the

f

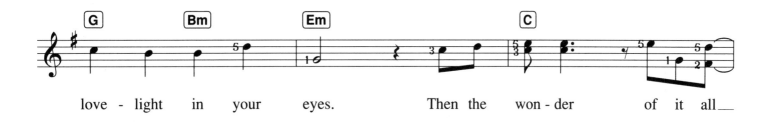

love - light in your eyes. Then the won - der of it all___

___ is that you just don't re - a - lize how much___ I

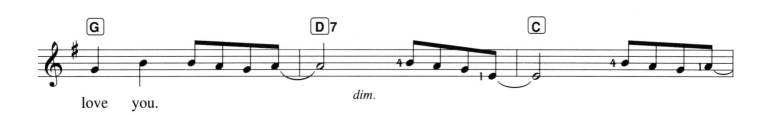

love you.

dim.

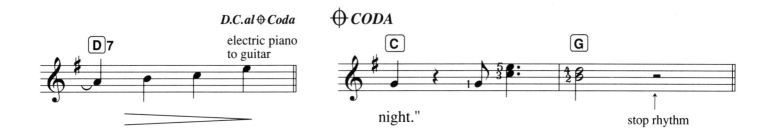

D.C. al ⊕ Coda

⊕ CODA

electric piano
to guitar

night."

stop rhythm

11

TOO YOUNG

Words by Sylvia Dee
Music by Sid Lippman

Suggested registration: saxophone
Rhythm: bossa nova
Tempo: medium (♩ = 104)

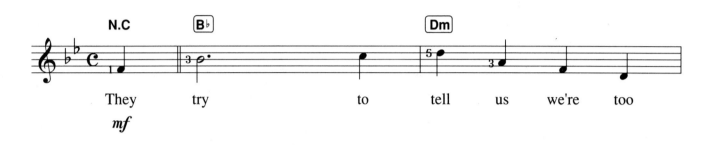

They   try   to   tell   us   we're   too

mf

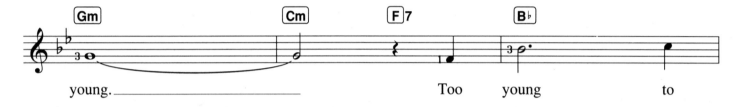

young. _____   Too   young   to

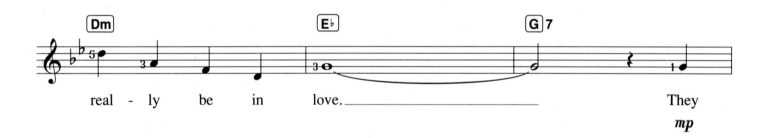

real - ly   be   in   love. _____   They

mp

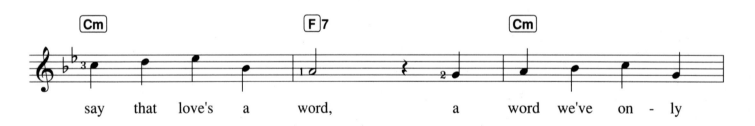

say   that   love's   a   word,   a   word   we've   on - ly

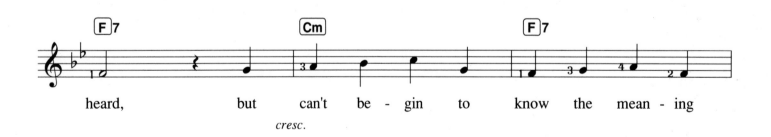

heard,   but   can't   be - gin   to   know   the   mean - ing

cresc.

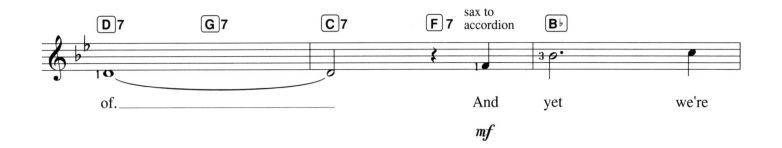

of._____ And yet we're

mf

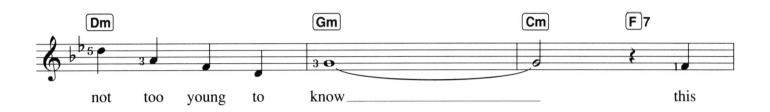

not too young to know_____ this

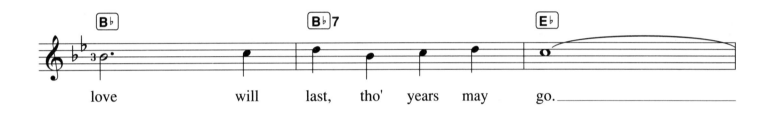

love will last, tho' years may go._____

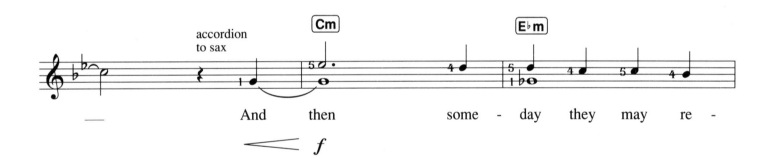

__ And then some - day they may re -

f

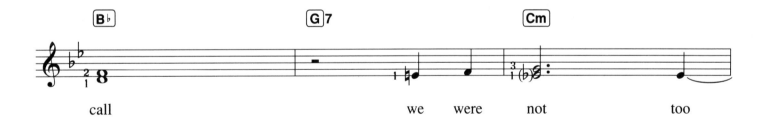

call we were not too

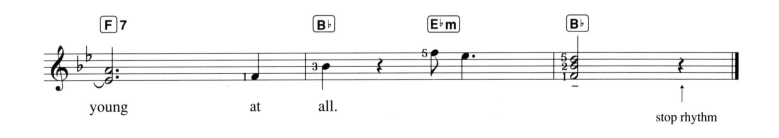

young at all. stop rhythm

SOMETIMES WHEN WE TOUCH

Words & Music by Dan Hill & Barry Mann

Suggested registration: electric piano
Rhythm: rock (or bossa nova)
Tempo: slow (♩ = 84)

VERSE

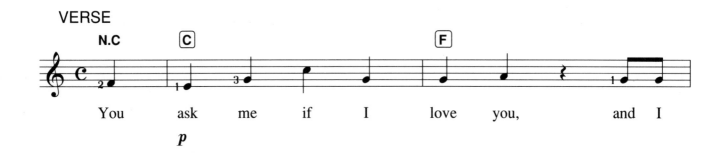

You ask me if I love you, and I

p

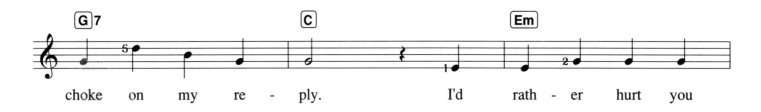

choke on my re - ply. I'd rath - er hurt you

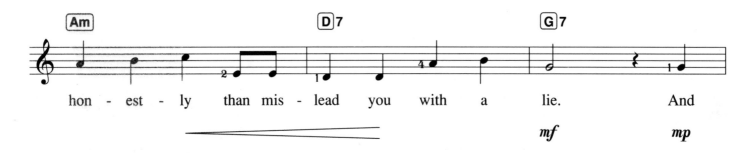

hon - est - ly than mis - lead you with a lie. And

mf *mp*

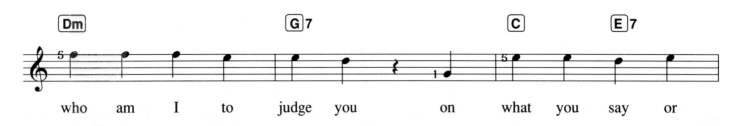

who am I to judge you on what you say or

do? I'm on - ly just be - gin - ning to

cresc.

see the real_____ you. And some-times when we

touch the hon - est - y's too much. And I

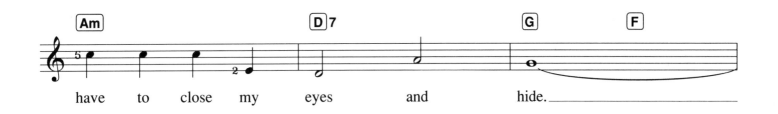

have to close my eyes and hide._____

___ I wan - na hold you till I die, till we

both break down and cry, I wan - na hold you till the

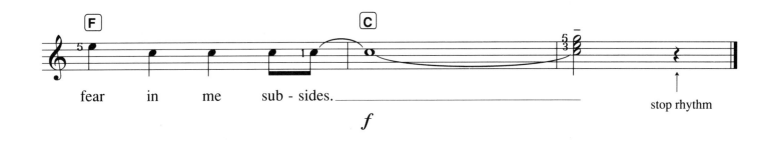

fear in me sub - sides._____

WHEN YOU'RE YOUNG AND IN LOVE

Words & Music by Van McCoy

Suggested registration: saxophone
Rhythm: rock
Tempo: medium (♩ = 100)

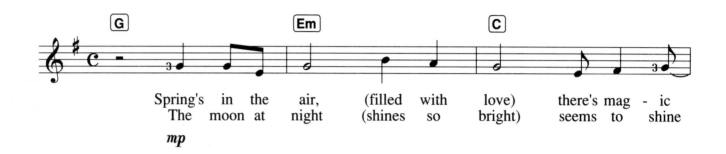

Spring's in the air, (filled with love) there's mag - ic
The moon at night (shines so bright) seems to shine

mp

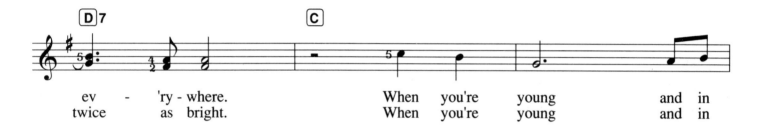

ev - 'ry - where. When you're young and in
twice as bright. When you're young and in

love._____ Life seems to
love._____ Dreams can come

be (just a dream) a world of fan - ta - sy.
true (try a dream) if you be - lieve they do.

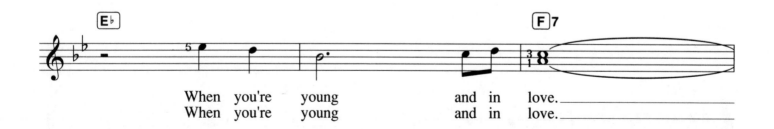

When you're young and in love._____
When you're young and in love._____

THE LOOK OF LOVE

Words by Hal David
Music by Burt Bacharach

Suggested registration: flute
Rhythm: rock
Tempo: medium (♩ = 116)

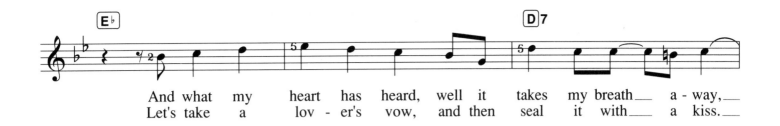

And what my heart has heard, well it takes my breath a-way,
Let's take a lov-er's vow, and then seal it with a kiss.

I can hard-ly wait to hold you, feel my arms a-round you,

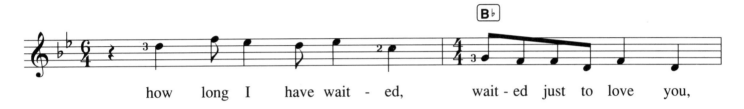

how long I have wait - ed, wait - ed just to love you,

flute to
muted trumpet

muted trumpet
to flute

1.   2.

now that I have found you, you've got the look — don't ev - er

mp   dim.

go, don't ev - er go,

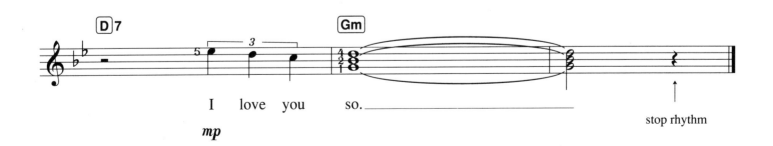

I love you so.

mp   stop rhythm

19

I'LL BE YOUR LOVER, TOO

Words & Music by Van Morrison

Suggested registration: guitar
Rhythm: rock
Tempo: medium (♩ = 96)

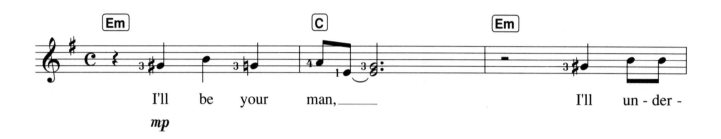

I'll be your man,_____ I'll un - der -

mp

stand._____ Do my best to take good care of

you. Yes, I will. You'll be_____

___ my queen, I'll be your king._____

And I'll be your_____ lov - er too._____

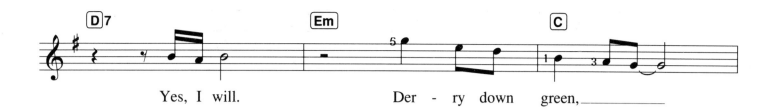

Yes, I will. Der - ry down green,_____

col - or of my dream,___ a dream that's

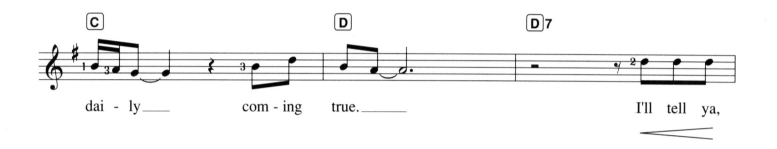

dai - ly___ com - ing true._____ I'll tell ya,

guitar to
string ensemble

when day is through, I will come to
you'll look at me_____ with eyes that

mf

you and tell you of your___ man - y
see, and melt in - to each oth - er's

D.C and Fade

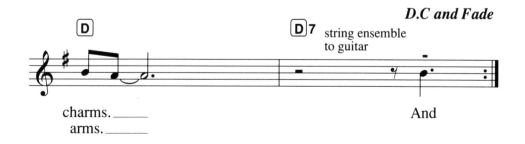

string ensemble
to guitar

charms._____ And
arms._____

THE FIRST TIME EVER I SAW YOUR FACE

Words & Music by Ewan MacColl

Suggested registration: french horn
Rhythm: rock
Tempo: slow (♩ = 80)

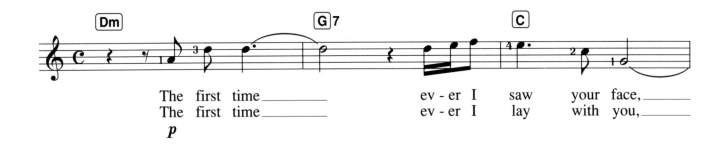

The first time_____ ev - er I saw your face,_____
The first time_____ ev - er I lay with you,_____

p

_____ I thought the sun_____ rose_____
_____ and felt your heart_____ so_____

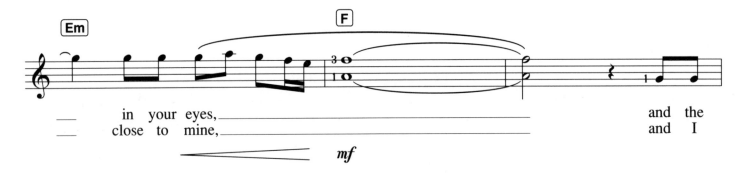

_____ in your eyes,_____ and the
_____ close to mine,_____ and I

mf

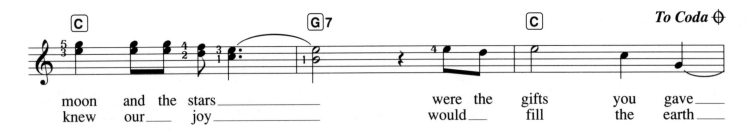

To Coda ⊕

moon and the stars_____ were the gifts you gave_____
knew our___ joy_____ would___ fill the earth

_____ to_____ the dark, _____ and the emp - ty

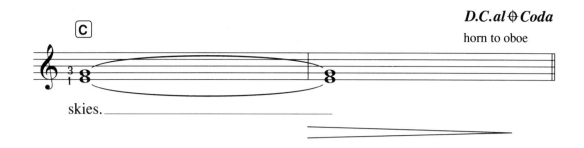

D.C.al ⊕ Coda

horn to oboe

skies.

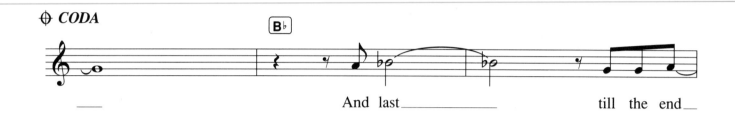

⊕ CODA

And last_____ till the end__

oboe to horn

__ of time,   my love.   The first time_____

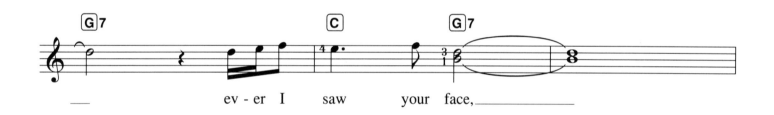

__   ev - er I   saw   your face,_____

your face,__   your face,__   your face,__

dim.

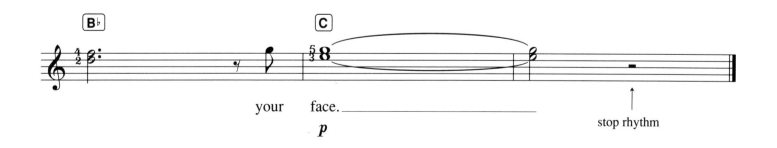

your   face._____

p

stop rhythm

IF NOT FOR YOU

Words & Music by Bob Dylan

Suggested registration: clarinet
Rhythm: rock
Tempo: medium (♩ = 108)

If not for you my sky would fall, rain would gath - er too._

mp

_ With - out your love, I'd be no - where at all.

cresc.

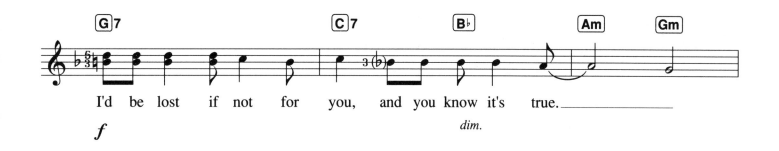

I'd be lost if not for you, and you know it's true._____

f   *dim.*

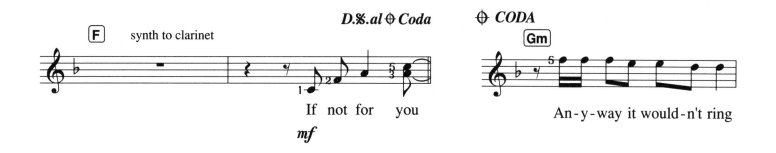

synth to clarinet   *D.%.al ⊕ Coda*   ⊕ *CODA*

If not for you   An - y - way it would - n't ring

mf

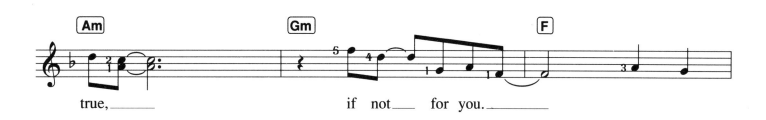

true,_____   if not___ for you._____

(Repeat and fade)

If not for you._____   If not for you.

WHAT THE WORLD NEEDS NOW IS LOVE

Words by Hal David
Music by Burt Bacharach

Suggested registration: trumpet
Rhythm: jazz waltz
Tempo: quite fast (♩ = 132)

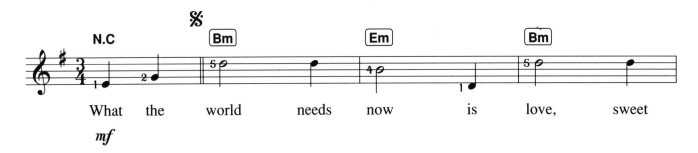

What the world needs now is love, sweet

love. It's the on - ly thing _____ that there's

just too lit - tle of. What the world needs

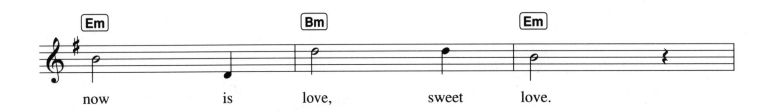

now is love, sweet love.

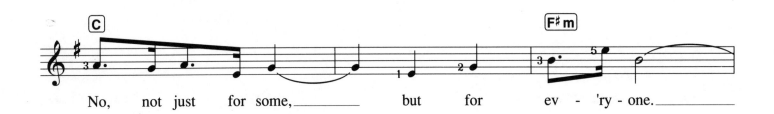

No, not just for some, _____ but for ev - 'ry - one. _____

Lord, we don't need a - noth - er moun - tain.

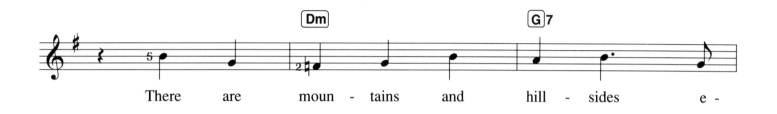

There are moun - tains and hill - sides e -

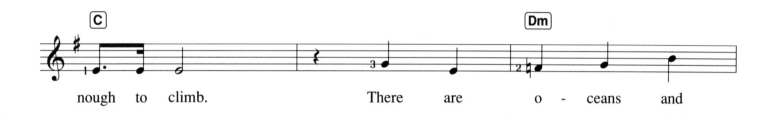

nough to climb. There are o - ceans and

riv - ers e - nough to cross, _____ e - nough to last

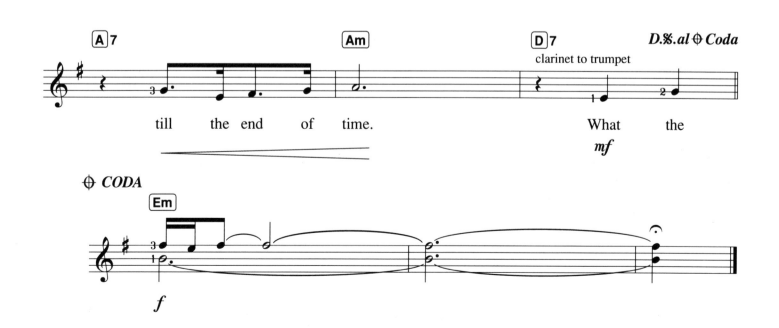

till the end of time. What the

⊕ CODA

MORE THAN I CAN SAY

Words & Music by Sonny Curtis & Jerry Allison

Suggested registration: guitar
Rhythm: rock
Tempo: medium (♩ = 112)

Oh,— oh,— yea,— yea!— I love you more than I— can

mf

say.— I'll love you twice as much to - mor - row,— oh,—

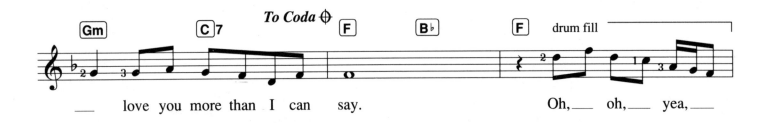

— love you more than I can say. Oh,— oh,— yea,—

yea!— I miss you ev - 'ry sin - gle day.—

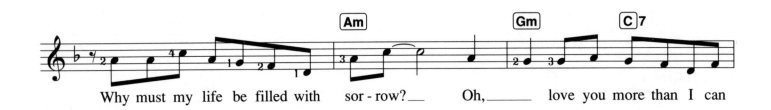

Why must my life be filled with sor - row?— Oh,— love you more than I can

say.   Don't you know I need you   so?_____

mp

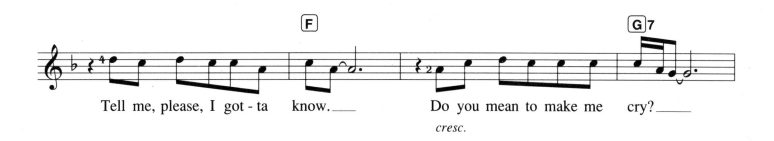

Tell me, please, I got - ta   know.___   Do you mean to make me   cry?_____

cresc.

piano to guitar   **D.%.al ⊕ Coda**

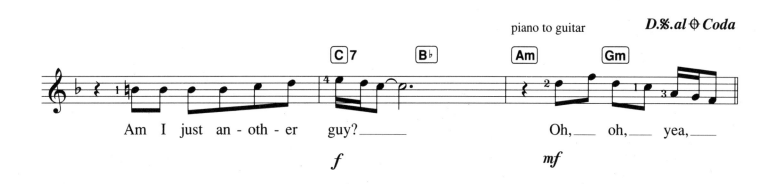

Am I just an - oth - er   guy?_____   Oh,___ oh,___ yea,___

f   *mf*

⊕ CODA

say.   I love you more than I can   say.

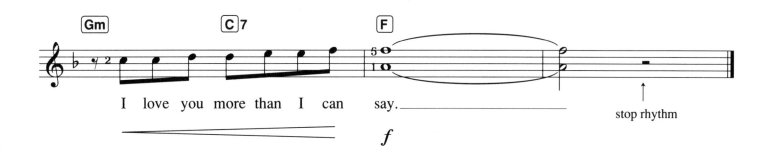

I love you more than I can   say._____

f   stop rhythm

IT'S IMPOSSIBLE (SOMOS NOVIOS)

Words by Sid Wayne
Music by A. Manzanero

Suggested registration: piano
Rhythm: bossa nova
Tempo: quite slow (♩ = 84)

pos - si - ble. Can the o - cean ___ keep from

rush - ing to the shore? It's just im - pos - si - ble. ___ If I

had you, ___ could I ev - er want for more? It's just im - pos - si - ble. ___

___ And to - mor - row, ___ should you ask me for the world, some - how I'd

get it. ___ I would sell my ve - ry soul, and not re - gret it, ___ for to

live with - out your love is just im - pos - si - ble.

LAY, LADY, LAY

Words & Music by Bob Dylan

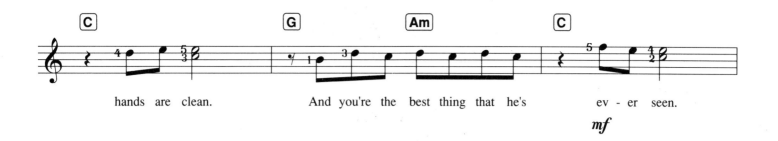

hands are clean. And you're the best thing that he's ev - er seen.

mf

Stay, la - dy, stay,___ stay with your man___ a - while.

p *mf*

Why wait an - y long - er for the world to be - gin?___ You can have your cake and eat it too._

mp *cresc.*

___ Why wait an - y long - er for the one you love,___ when he's

mf *cresc.*

D.C. al ⊕ Coda   ⊕ CODA

cut flute

stand - ing in front of you?_____ Stay, la - dy, stay,___

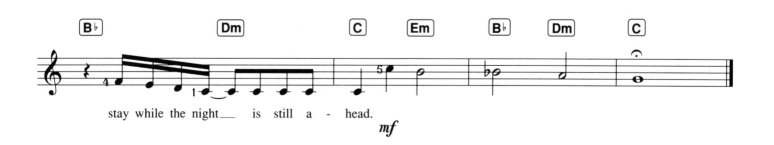

stay while the night___ is still a - head.

mf

MY KIND OF GIRL

Words & Music by Leslie Bricusse

Suggested registration: piano
Rhythm: swing
Tempo: medium (♩ = 112)

CLAUDETTE

Words & Music by Roy Orbison

Suggested registration: jazz organ (with tremolo)
Rhythm: rock (or twist)
Tempo: medium (♩ = 120)

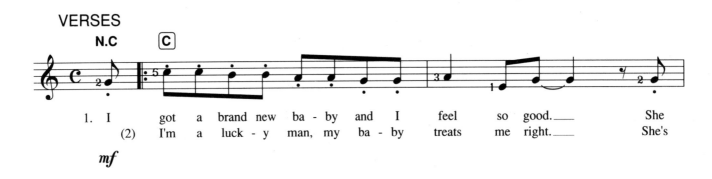

I've ev - er met, I get the best___ lov - ing that I'll ev - er get from Clau -

dette. Pret - ty lit - tle pet, Clau - dette.

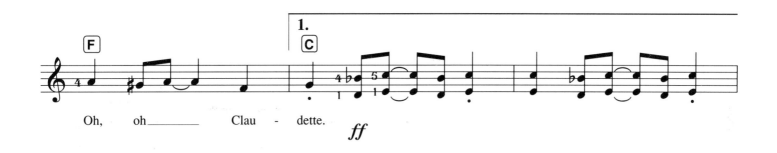

1.

Oh, oh_____ Clau - dette. *ff*

2.

2. Well *mf* dette. *ff*

stop rhythm

TRY A LITTLE TENDERNESS

Words & Music by Harry Woods, Jimmy Campbell & Reg Connelly

Suggested registration: piano
Rhythm: swing
Tempo: fairly slow (♩ = 76)

MASTER CHORD CHART

C
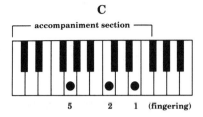

Cm
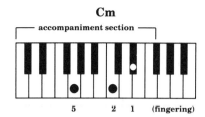

C7
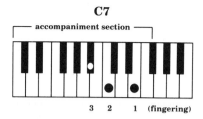

D♭
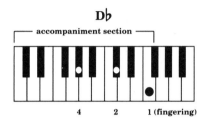

C♯m
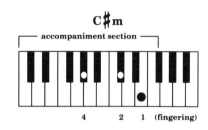

D♭(C♯)7
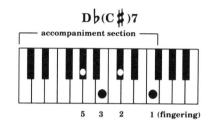

D
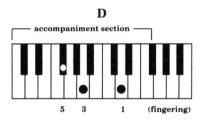

Dm
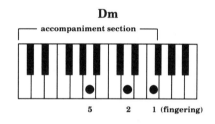

D7
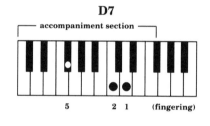

E♭
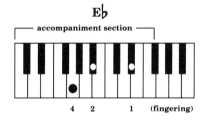

E♭m
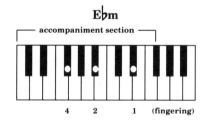

E♭7
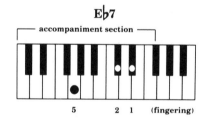

E
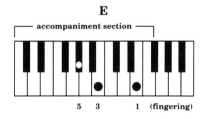

Em
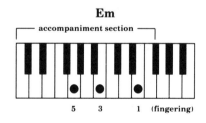

E7
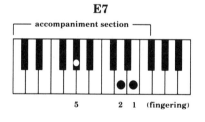

F
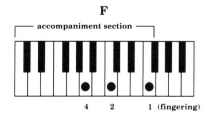

Fm
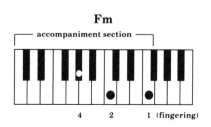

F7
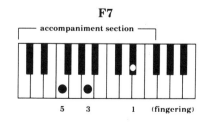

MASTER CHORD CHART

G♭(F♯)
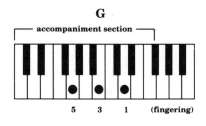
5   3   1   (fingering)

F♯m
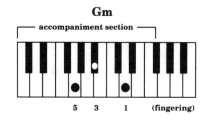
5   3   1   (fingering)

G♭(F♯)7
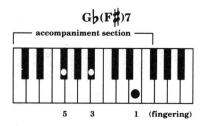
5   3   1   (fingering)

G
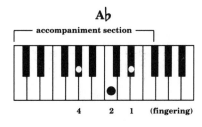
5   3   1   (fingering)

Gm
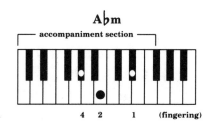
5   3   1   (fingering)

G7
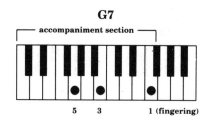
5   3   1 (fingering)

A♭
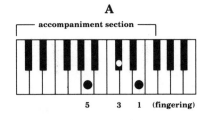
4   2   1   (fingering)

A♭m
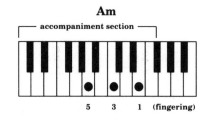
4   2   1   (fingering)

A♭7
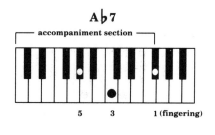
5   3   1 (fingering)

A
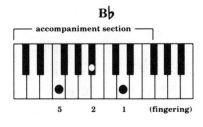
5   3   1 (fingering)

Am
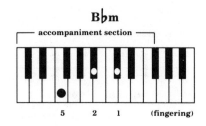
5   3   1   (fingering)

A7
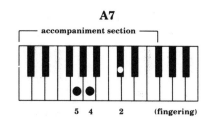
5   4   2   (fingering)

B♭
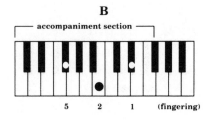
5   2   1   (fingering)

B♭m
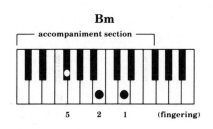
5   2   1   (fingering)

B♭7
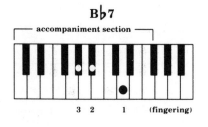
3   2   1   (fingering)

B
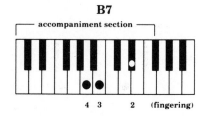
5   2   1   (fingering)

Bm
5   2   1   (fingering)

B7
4   3   2   (fingering)

14620 11/92